WONDERDOG

WONDERDOG

Everything your dog

wanted to learn

but was afraid to ask

Dr Katrina Warren

HarperCollins*Publishers*

HarperCollins*Publishers*

First published in Australia in 2001
Reprinted in 2001 (twice), 2002
by HarperCollins*Publishers* Pty Limited
ABN 36 009 913 517
A member of the HarperCollins*Publishers* (Australia) Pty Limited Group
www.harpercollins.com.au

HarperCollins*Publishers*
25 Ryde Road, Pymble, Sydney, NSW 2073, Australia
31 View Road, Glenfield, Auckland 10, New Zealand
77-85 Fulham Palace Road, London W6 8JB, United Kingdom
Hazelton Lanes, 55 Avenue Road, Suite 2900, Toronto, Ontario M5R 3L2
and 1995 Markham Road, Scarborough, Ontario M1B 5M8, Canada
10 East 53rd Street, New York NY 10022, USA

National Library of Australia Cataloguing-in-Publication data:

Katrina Warren.
   Wonderdog: everything your dog wanted to learn
   but was afraid to ask.
   ISBN 0 7322 6951 2.
   1. Dogs – Training. I. Title.
636.70835

Cover and internal photography by Mark Bramley
Internal illustrations by Deborah Clarke
Cover and internal design by Judi Rowe, HarperCollins Design Studio
Printed and bound in China by Everbest Printing Co Ltd on 100gsm White Offset

8 7 6 5 4   02 03 04 05

Acknowledgements

Thanks to:

Joan Bray, for breeding such a beautiful puppy.

Mark Morrissey and David Sheridan, for believing in this project.

Craig, for coping.

Toby thanks:

His minders – Sue, Mike, Ilona, Mikey, Justine, Ken, Tom, Narelle, and Dan.

His canine pals – Benny, Bowie, Hannah, Teddy, Ren, and Andy.

When in Melbourne, Toby loves to shop at The House of Cats and Dogs and in Sydney, he chooses Dogue.

Foreword

Just over five years ago, Katrina asked me if I would like to assist her in selecting a puppy to be her pet and companion. After much research and deliberation of Katrina's lifestyle, we chose a lovely litter of Border Collie puppies in the Southern Highlands of NSW. We were now faced with the daunting task of selecting which puppy was to become Toby The Wonderdog. The litter consisted of seven equally gorgeous puppies, but one chocolate and white male puppy repeatedly came to the forefront and our increasing attention. He was outgoing, extremely friendly with a confident manner —the attributes that I had advised Katrina she should be seeking in a puppy.

As time has shown, this selection, of course, was the right one. Toby has now become a national television celebrity — popular with children and adults alike.

In this book, Katrina outlines the training methods she applied to Toby, in a simple, easy-to-understand, step-by-step manner. The methods that Katrina has used have shown that she not only understands the physiological workings of dogs, but also has an excellent understanding of their pack instincts and psychological needs. As a professional dog trainer, I would recommend this book to all dog owners and up-and-coming dog trainers as it shows not only how to train your dog, but also how to have good, old fashioned fun and enjoyment with your dog.

To Katrina and Toby, congratulations on a job well done!

Steve Austin

Contents

WONDERDOG TRICKS

WONDERDOG TIPS

Introduction

Toby and I have been a team for five years now and I have spent more time with him than most people I know. During that time we have formed a very special bond and I try to return to him as much love and pleasure as he gives me.

I have one of the best jobs in the world — I get paid to work with animals and that also involves bringing my dog to work most days of the week. Toby has actually grown up on national television and the number of people who have followed his career constantly amazes me. I am regularly questioned about his breed, his diet and his temperament, but most often I am asked how I trained him to be obedient and perform tricks. In this book I will show you how I taught Toby his tricks.

Training Toby began from the moment I took him home. I socialised him, took him to puppy preschool and made an effort to spend as much time as possible with him. Dogs respond really well to positive praise and that's what I gave him plenty of. I showered him with praise whenever he was a good boy for *anything* — sitting quietly, chewing his own toys, or weeing on the grass. I also used food treats to reward him because I found he was very motivated by food. You need to figure out just what motivates your individual dog — it may be food, his favourite toy or the sound of your voice praising him. I still use food rewards whenever I start teaching a new trick, to get Toby enthusiastic, but once he has conquered his task I vary the rewards with toys, as I don't want him to expect food every time he does something right.

I don't believe that dogs should be smacked or hit — they don't understand and will only become scared of you. The most punishment Toby receives is a firm 'No!' and occasionally I ignore him if he is behaving inappropriately.

There are several factors but no secrets involved in having your own Wonderdog and one of the most important is you must choose the right breed to suit your lifestyle. I am very conscious of people choosing a Border Collie to have their own 'Toby Dog' without realising that Toby is a highly active dog who needs lots of physical and mental stimulation.

Please do some research into any breed that you are interested in, to make sure it will fit into your life for the next 15 years or so.

I enjoy seeing the happiness that Toby brings to others in his day-to-day life. Whether he visits schools, retirement homes or is doing a stage show, children and adults alike appear to be fascinated by my beautiful little dog. This is why I wanted to write this book — because with a little bit of knowledge, a little bit of patience and a lot of love directed the right way, I believe that everyone can get as much enjoyment from their relationship with their dog as I do with Toby.

Katrina

Toby the Wonderdog

Toby the Wonderdog was born on 19 February 1996, in the Southern Highlands of New South Wales. The brightest of a litter of seven Border Collies, he easily caught my eye as I was on the lookout for a TV co-host. It was a combination of his unusual chocolate-brown markings and his extroverted nature that made him The One.

Even before he hit the big smoke, Toby knew he was destined for fame. After all, TV cameras had already filmed me choosing him from the litter for 'Totally Wild' on Network Ten. From then on, everything from his first bath to his vaccinations and his encounters with sheep was documented. A star was born.

Toby posed for his first magazine spread at the tender age of 10 weeks, turning it on for the cameras as if he had been bred for the role. Since then he has graced the pages of *New Weekly*, *Woman's Day*, *New Idea*, *Dolly*, *That's Life!* and *Australian Good Taste*. Now an experienced cover-dog, he has also clocked up several covers of *Dog's Life!*,

Pets, Vets 'n' People, *Looksmart*, *Aussie Post* as well as numerous
TV guides around the country.

Seasoned TV hosts spotted his natural flair, inviting him to make
guest appearances on 'Good Morning Australia', '11AM' and
'Denise'. His popularity soared with his move to the prime time hit
show 'Harry's Practice'. Most weeks he co-presents segments with
me on all aspects of dog care.

When he's not filming, The Wonderdog — as he's been dubbed by
his adoring fans — has a hectic schedule. A typical week involves
radio interviews (he barks his answers), making guest appearances
and signing 'pawgraphs'. He is booked for many shopping centre and
Pet Expo appearances where he performs tricks on stage and
entertains people of all ages. He has MCed a Wiggles concert and
also co-presented a segment at the 'People's Choice Awards' which
was telecast live across Australia. Never one to knock back a worthy
cause, Toby also finds time to support his favourite charity, The
Assistance Dogs for Independence.

Toby currently lives in a leafy, dog-friendly Sydney suburb. He relaxes
after work with a game of Frisbee in the park (in summer he loves a
surf), followed by a juicy bone while he answers his fan mail.

Wonderdog Essential Commands

There are a few basic commands that are essential for your dog to know before he can attempt the tricks in this book. These commands will be frequently used throughout and they are **SIT**, **DROP**, **STAY** and **COME**.

It is much easier to teach these at puppy age than to teach an adult dog who is set in his ways. However, you can teach an old dog new tricks — it just takes a little more time and patience.

From the time a puppy enters your house you can start training him up to be a Wonderdog. In fact, the first few months of a pup's life are a crucial time in developing his dog skills. This is the time when a pup learns all about the world — things like how to behave socially around people and other animals, what is right and wrong, and what really pleases you.

Puppies have so much energy and you can channel some of this into short bursts of productive training. Pups learn from positive experiences and that is the way I have trained Toby. Everything I teach him is fun and is rewarded with praise, treats and toys. And he responds because he genuinely enjoys pleasing me (plus he gets a treat as well).

I encourage all puppies to go to puppy preschool. This is a series of classes for puppies from 8 to 16 weeks of age where they learn socialisation skills as well as basic manners. These classes are run by dog trainers or vets who will give you plenty of advice on raising a healthy pup as well as how to train him with positive reinforcement.

Wonderdog Essential Hand Signals

Use these signals to reinforce your spoken commands.

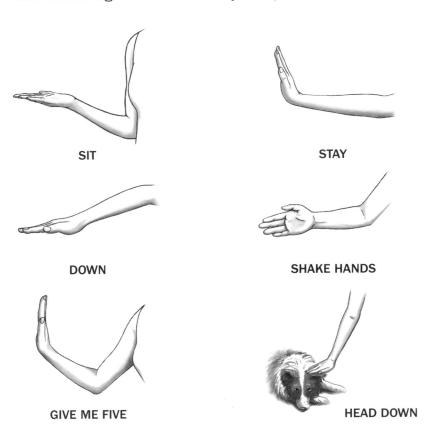

SIT

STAY

DOWN

SHAKE HANDS

GIVE ME FIVE

HEAD DOWN

SPEAK (1)

SPEAK (2)

TAKE A BOW (1)

TAKE A BOW (2)

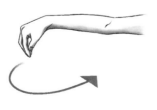

CHASE TAIL

CRAWL

1. Sit

SIT is the most basic command that all dogs should know. It allows you to take control of your dog as well as keep him still to examine him, groom him, give tablets etc.
If your dog sits when told, then you have the basics for good manners around people and food, as well as the prerequisite for tricks like **BEG** and **SHAKE**.

WHAT YOU NEED

★ A hungry dog — best before mealtime
★ A quiet room with no distractions   ★ Some treats

WONDERDOG STEPS

1 Attract your dog's attention with a food treat while he is standing.

2 Hold the treat above his nose and gently lift upwards and backwards, keeping the food in direct contact with your dog's nose as he tilts his head backwards.

3 Most dogs will naturally move into the **SIT** position. You can also help out by gently pushing his backside down whilst you hold the treat over his nose with your other hand.

4 Say **'SIT'** as soon as he starts moving into position. Immediately reward him with the treat and praise.

5 Repeat 10 to 12 times a session and always before mealtime.

6 Once mastered, start practising with distractions, always rewarding and showering him with praise as soon as he **SITS**.

7 If you find your dog jumping up for the food, don't get cross. Just say a gentle **'NO!'** and start again. The most important thing is to learn to ignore him when he doesn't get it right (i.e. no fuss and no treats!) and really let him know when he is pleasing you.

8 To continue the training, begin asking your dog to **SIT** before any action or event – i.e. before meals, before you put his leash on, before you both walk out the door. Only when your dog **SITS** quietly do you proceed. This will help elevate you to 'leader of the pack' status and your dog will learn to respect your requests right from the beginning.

★ TOBY'S TIP ★

'I learn much more quickly and am more motivated when the food reward I am being offered is something really tasty, like tiny pieces of chicken or cabanossi, rather than boring dry food.'

2. Drop/Down

A preliminary command to learn **BANG** or **CRAWL**, this command can also be used to put your dog into a submissive situation at any time.

WHAT YOU NEED

★ A dog who **SITS**

★ Treats

WONDERDOG STEPS

1 Tell your dog to **'SIT'**. Reward him with a treat.

2 Hold the treat in front of your dog's nose and slowly move it towards the ground. As he reaches for the treat, slide it along the ground in an L-shaped movement.

3 You must keep contact between the treat and your dog's nose, and his body should naturally follow.

4 Apply slight pressure on your dog's shoulders and gently push him towards the ground.

5 Use the command **'DOWN'** and as soon as he is down, reward with the treat.

6 If your dog is not responding, you can help him physically by lifting his front legs out in front of him. Do this gently, and reassure him with your voice. Repeat this step several times until he becomes confident with the movement. Then go back to Step 4, which your dog should find easier now.

7 Start including a hand signal of a downward stroke each time you say **'DOWN'**.

8 Once your dog has mastered **DOWN** from the **SIT** position, you can start to teach him from the **STAND** position, or even from walking. The hand signal movement will be clear to your dog even from a distance.

★ TOBY'S TIP ★

'At the end of each command you must give me a release word such as "OK", so I know that I can relax and get back to my own business. It also becomes the magic reward word at the end of training to tell me I have been a good dog.'

3. Stay

A necessity for any Wonderdog so that you have control of him at all times. A smart dog learns that **STAY** means to hold whatever position he is in, whether it is **BEGGING**, **BOWING** or he is just **SITTING** waiting for dinner.

WHAT YOU NEED

★ A dog who **SITS**   ★ A lead
★ A confined area   ★ Treats

WONDERDOG STEPS

1 Put your dog on a lead and stand next to him.
Command him to **'SIT'**, and don't move.

2 When he is still, say **'STAY'** and reward him only
while he is sitting still. Don't you move either.
If he moves from the **SIT** position, gently
place him back and start again.

3 Be patient and practise until your dog will **SIT** for a
minute by your side. Include a hand signal which is
an open palm each time you say **'STAY'**.
Don't overdo it. In the next training session
you can progress.

4 Have your dog **SIT** next to you and take a step back as you give the command to **'STAY'**. If he **SITS** on his mark, then you can immediately reward him with the treat. If he breaks the **SIT**, say a gentle **'NO!'** and move him back to the exact starting point each time.

5 Gradually increase your distance on the lead until you are confident that your dog has understood your request.

6 Gradually add distractions and shower him with praise when he doesn't move. Your dog has to grasp the concept that moving is the wrong thing to do in this case and that you are really happy when he stays still.

7 Once mastered on the lead (it will take a few sessions), you can commence off the lead in confined areas of the house and garden. Remember that your puppy has a short attention span, so practise **STAY** for short periods of time only.

8 As he gets older you can practise leaving the room, making distractions and increasing the time required to **STAY**. If he moves, just put him back on the same spot with a firm **'STAY'** and start again (go back to using the lead if necessary).

★ TOBY'S TIP ★

'No matter how well we dogs behave at home, never assume that we will be as cooperative in an open space where there are distractions everywhere. I blame it on my working dog instinct — I love to chase moving things.'

4. The Recall

This essential command teaches your dog to come to you whenever you call. It is much easier to teach this to a puppy than an adult and there are certain breeds that can be more difficult to teach than others.

WHAT YOU NEED

★ A long lead ★ A very long rope
★ A squeaky toy ★ Treats

WONDERDOG STEPS

1 The key to this command is teaching your dog that coming to you is a pleasant experience. Of course he will want to come to you if he gets his favourite toy, some food and verbal praise from you when he does.

2 Start calling **'COME'** around meals and playtimes, always telling him what a good boy he is, even though he was going to come anyway.

3 Practise moving backwards and squeaking a toy, so your dog follows. Always include the command **'COME'** as you move.

'COME'

4 With your dog on a lead, tell him to **'SIT'** facing you. Step back and then call him to you. You can apply gentle pressure on the lead and move backwards so he will come towards you. Encourage him with a squeaky toy and verbal praise.

5 Progress to a longer rope, so he starts to **RECALL** from distances. Take this with you to the park and keep practising. Perfect the **RECALL** on the rope before considering letting him run free and when you do, be sure to do so in an enclosed area.

6 Start to include a hand signal of open arms with each command.

7 Always give lashings of praise, make a fuss, and let him have his toy or treat when he does come to you. You have to make yourself more exciting than the other dogs, trees and people in the park or why would your dog bother returning at all?

★ TOBY'S TIP ★

'Never punish us or scream at us if we don't come back. We're only doing our doggy stuff and that will teach us to be scared to come to you at all.
If we ignore you completely when called, you should retrieve us and start again on a rope.'

TOP TRAINING TIPS

1. Keep training sessions short. Remember, a dog has an attention span like a small child, so 10 minutes at a time is adequate or your dog may lose interest.

2. Always make training a positive experience and end on a happy note, by having a quick game or giving him a favourite toy. Don't train your dog if you are in a bad mood as you won't be giving the right energy, and you are more likely to lose your temper.

3. As frustrating as it can be if your dog has done something naughty, never lose your temper or hit him. He won't understand what he has done and it will only make him scared of you.

4. Consistency is the key — all members of the house must agree to the same rules, key words and hand signals. When learning tricks, repetition is essential. Teach each trick over at least a week, building up gradually so your dog can build up his confidence in what you are asking — *don't rush*!

5. Buy yourself a bumbag — these are fabulous for training as you can put things like your food treats and house keys in them and free up your hands.

6. Start training as soon as you bring home a puppy. Puppies are most impressionable during the first 16 weeks of life and this is the time to teach them as many dos and don'ts as possible.

7. You *can* teach an old dog new tricks, you just need a little more time and patience. Dogs of any age will respond to training, and the mental stimulation is always good for them.

8. If you are using food treats, make sure they are something that smells really good to your dog and he will be a lot keener to figure out what you want him to do. For example, small pieces of cheese, chicken or cabanossi have Toby a lot more excited than his everyday dry food.

9. Put aside an hour each week for training classes. These not only help with basic obedience, but teach your dog social skills as well. In order to teach the tricks in this book, your dog must understand the basic commands of **SIT**, **STAY**, **DROP** and **COME**.

10. Think of training as fun. The more you train your dog the more pleasurable his company will be.

Wonderdog Tricks

TRICK 1
Beg

This is always a party pleaser. Your dog sits up on his haunches and begs for food or his favourite toy. Smart dogs (like Toby) actually learn that they receive attention when in this pose and start doing it whenever a new guest has food.

WHAT YOU NEED

★ A dog who can **SIT** and **STAY**   ★ Treats

WONDERDOG STEPS

1 Put your dog in a **SIT** position.

2 Hold a treat above his nose and as he reaches for it, gradually lift the treat a little higher. Keep his attention on the treat by not lifting it too quickly.

3 As he lifts his front legs off the ground, say **'BEG'** and reward him with the treat and verbal praise. He must learn to take food only on your command for this trick to be successful.

4 Repeat these steps several times, assisting your dog with his balance as necessary (this is an unnatural position for a dog, so he might need some help). Try allowing him to rest his front legs on your forearm. He may only need you to hold one leg.

5 Once your dog has grasped the concept of sitting on his hindquarters tell him to **'STAY'** and reward him as he holds the position, even if he only manages it for a second at first. Always step in as necessary to help him balance.

6 Gradually increase the time he holds the **BEG** position.

7 Always remember to give your dog the release word **'OK'** when he is finished.

8 Once your dog has mastered the command and can hold the position, you can start to increase your distance from him when you give the command.

★ **TOBY'S TIP** ★

'When Katrina first started to teach me this trick, I used to get excited and would jump up for the treat. Katrina would ignore me when I did this, but reward me when I balanced on my haunches. I never got the treat when I tried to grab it.'

TRICK 2
Shake Hands

This teaches your dog to make human friends quickly by shaking hands to say 'hello'.

What really impresses people is when your dog actually knows his right from his left paw.

WHAT YOU NEED

★ A dog who **SITS**   ★ Treats

WONDERDOG STEPS

1 Tell your dog to **'SIT'**.

2 Then get down to his level and kneel before him.

3 Hold your right hand palm up, and reach over for your dog's right paw, reassuring him as you gently pick it up (scratching behind the paw helps).

4 Encourage your dog by telling him **'YES'** and then command **'SHAKE'** as you softly shake his paw.

5 Reward your dog with a treat, even though it is you doing all the work at this point. You are really rewarding him for his cooperation, while teaching him you want to hold his paw.

6 Once he is used to you saying the **'SHAKE'** command and lifting his paw, try hesitating and he will probably offer his paw to you as he knows that he'll get a treat. Catch his paw as soon as he starts to lift it and help him out, always saying **'SHAKE'** and always rewarding him.

7 Don't forget to give him the release word **'OK'** when you have finished and put his paw back down.

8 Once he has mastered this you can say **'SHAKE RIGHT'** when you lift the right paw.

9 Commence the whole process again with your left hand reaching across for his left paw while you say the command **'SHAKE LEFT'**. Help him as necessary until he realises he now has to lift the other paw. Repeat and reward as above. Do the left and right paws separately and don't try to do them together until your dog clearly understands what you are asking.

★ **TOBY'S TIP** ★
'I don't really know my right from left, I have just learnt to lift whichever paw Katrina holds her hand out to.'

TRICK 3
Give Me Five & Ten

This trick is very cute and is really just an altered version of **SHAKE**. You are teaching your dog to lift his paw in response to you holding your palm up to him. This time not the diagonal leg, but the one the same side as your hand.

WHAT YOU NEED

★ A dog who can **SHAKE** hands   ★ Treats

WONDERDOG STEPS

1 Kneel before your dog and offer your hand towards the leg directly in front of you.

2 Pick up your dog's paw, reassuring him.

3 Instead of shaking his paw, lay it flat on your palm and say **'GIVE ME FIVE'**. Reward him with a treat.

4 Practise until your dog is offering his paw to you when you offer him your palm near the ground.

5 Gradually turn your hand so it is facing your dog and start moving it up towards shoulder level. Your aim is to get your dog to reach up and tap your palm.

6 Practise with both right and left paws, using the **'GIVE ME FIVE'** command.

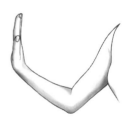

7 Once perfected with both individual paws, see what your dog does when you excitedly offer both palms and ask **'GIVE ME TEN'**. Some dogs will automatically try to give you both. Shower your dog with praise and encouragement at any attempt to lift either or both paws off the ground.

8 Your aim now is to get your dog to tap both of your palms with his paws. To help him understand what you want, ask him to **'GIVE YOU FIVE'**. Reward him with the treat while maintaining contact with his paw and gently lift the other paw off the ground, helping with his balance if necessary.

9 Keep practising over several sessions until your dog is attempting to give you both paws at once.

★ TOBY'S TIP ★

'I found it easy to learn **GIVE ME FIVE** with both the left and right paws, before attempting both paws at once. That way I had understood that I was to lift each paw to the corresponding hand, and it made sense that when both hands were presented I would lift both paws.'

TRICK 4
Jumping Through the Hoop

I use this trick in stage shows when I ask Toby to pick up his toy from the other side of the stage. He only needs a short run-up to jump quite high, and always gets lots of applause.

WHAT YOU NEED

★ A dog who will **SIT** and **STAY**   ★ A Hula-Hoop   ★ A favourite toy
★ A corridor   ★ A second person, if possible   ★ A lead

WONDERDOG STEPS

1 Have your helper hold the hoop at a right angle to the wall of the corridor. We use the wall as a barrier so your dog has no choice but to go in the direction you are asking.

2 With your dog on a lead make him **SIT** and **STAY** on one side of the hoop. Make him watch you as you put his favourite toy on the other side of the hoop.

3 Lead him through the hoop and let him have the toy on the other side. He probably won't even notice the hoop until you slowly start lifting it off the ground, making him jump a little.

4 As he lifts his feet to jump say the command **'THROUGH'** and then **'YES'** when he makes it through to retrieve his toy.

5 Remove the lead and repeat the above steps, always commencing with your dog in the **SIT** and **STAY** positions.

6 Once the hoop is a certain height you may find your dog choosing to go under rather than through it. If he does, ignore him and return to the starting point. Lower the hoop and start again, lifting it only one centimetre each attempt.

7 Practise in the corridor, so he is always confined by walls, before attempting the trick in any open space. When you do venture somewhere else, start on a lead again until you are confident that he understands the task.

8 You can also teach your dog to jump through your arms. Basically you just follow the above steps, slowly replacing the hoop with your arms held to form a circle. Obviously, small dogs should not be expected to jump very high.

★ TOBY'S TIP ★

'Now that I understand what 'THROUGH' means, I love to jump through agility equipment, boxes or anything else I am asked. The size of your dog is a very important consideration here — sometimes I find it a tight squeeze fitting through Katrina's arms, so be careful.'

TRICK 5
Speak & Count

Teaching your dog to **SPEAK** (bark on command) can be very impressive. Toby now barks in response to a very slight movement from me, which means that I can make it look like he is barking to answer questions. I may ask, 'Toby, what is three plus four?' and he counts the answer.

WHAT YOU NEED
★ A favourite toy ★ Treats

WONDERDOG STEPS

1 You must first figure out what it is that triggers your dog to bark — perhaps it is excitement at seeing his favourite toy or maybe it is when there is someone at the door. You need to be able to anticipate his barking.

2 Set your dog up in a situation where you know he will bark. As he does, excitedly say **'SPEAK'** followed by **'GOOD BOY'** and reward him with a treat or his toy (if that's what made him bark).

3 Repeat the above step a few times. Most dogs enjoy being rewarded for barking and pick this up quite quickly.

4 Start incorporating a hand signal with your verbal command and keep on practising.

5 Next, command **'QUIET'** and give a Shhh! hand signal. Reward your dog with the treat or toy as soon as he stops barking.
You want him to learn that he barks only until you stop your signal.

6 You can help your dog out by gently holding his muzzle closed with your hand, while telling him **'QUIET'**, followed by **'GOOD BOY'** and then give the reward.

7 You will also find that if you hold a food treat to your dog's nose as you say **'QUIET'**, he will stop barking in order to sniff. Reward him as soon as he is quiet.

8 Practise while you are nearby and then gradually start moving further away from your dog. Always make sure you have your dog's full attention so that he is watching your hand signals.

9 Now you can teach your dog to count. Firstly, command only one bark before saying **'QUIET'**. Practise doing one bark until you are sure he understands that one hand signal means one bark.

10 As you give the hand signal, also nod your head once and don't forget to reward him with a treat and praise.

11 Once your dog knows one hand signal and one nod equals one bark, try doing two hand signals with two head nods. Basically, you are asking him to **'SPEAK, SPEAK'** but without the words.

12 Practise counting from one to two, gradually removing the hand signals and using nods only. With time, you can reduce that nod to the slightest movement or even a blink.

13 As soon as your dog hits the target number applaud him by clapping or saying excitedly **'CLEVER BOY'**. That way, he has no reason to keep barking as he is already being praised. Once he knows to bark at your signal, getting him to count to ten is no more difficult for him than counting to two.

★ TOBY'S TIP ★

'When I was younger, I thought it was great to be rewarded just for barking. However, I got a little over-excited and carried away. Make sure you only practise this trick in a calm environment and only for short periods of time. The **QUIET** command is just as important as the **SPEAK** command.'

TRICK 6
Sad Face

We use this trick a lot when filming. It is the perfect face for when Toby is supposed to be sad, lonely, jealous or staring at his bowl of food.

WHAT YOU NEED

★ A dog who will **DROP**

★ A dog who will **STAY**   ★ Treats

WONDERDOG STEPS

1 Begin with your dog in the **DROP/DOWN** position.
Make sure his front legs are out in front.

2 Let him see a treat in your hand and place this
hand on the ground in front of the dog's nose.

3 Don't let him grab the food but gently hold
his head down to the ground saying
'HEAD DOWN'.

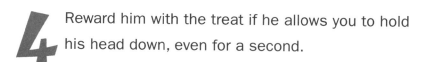

4 Reward him with the treat if he allows you to hold
his head down, even for a second.

5 Make him learn that if you hold his head down, he will get a reward (*never* try and force a dog, though).

6 Now start commanding him to **'STAY'** in position without you holding his head on the floor. If he holds position, immediately give him the release word of **'OK'** and reward him with a treat.

7 Practise by asking him to **'STAY'** for longer periods of time and from further away.

8 If he does put his head up, just say a firm **'NO!'** and place his head back down and start again.

9 Start including hand signals when you give the **'HEAD DOWN'** command.

★ **TOBY'S TIP** ★

'It is very important that you give me the release word "OK" when I am allowed to put my head back up. Otherwise, I will think you want me to stay like that. I will inevitably break the position from boredom, which is not a good training method. I really like to hear the "OK" word as it means I have got it right and Katrina is happy.'

TRICK 7
Bang

This is where you point your fingers like a gun at your dog and say **'BANG'**. Your dog falls to the ground and plays dead.

The key here is to take your time and not expect to put it all together at once.

WHAT YOU NEED
★ A dog who **SITS, STAYS** and **DROPS**   ★ Treats

WONDERDOG STEPS

1 Begin with your dog in the **DROP** position and reward him with a treat.

2 Gently roll him onto his back, reassuring him and helping him with his balance. Reward him for his cooperation.

3 Start again. As you roll him onto his back, say **'BANG'** and then reward him with the treat.

4 Keep practising until your dog naturally rolls onto his back from the **DROP** position when he hears the command **'BANG'**.

5 Start including a hand signal of fingers pointing like a gun.

6 Once perfected from the **DROP** position, commence from the **SIT** position. You may have to physically give your dog a helping hand to make him realise he has to **SIT** then **DROP** then **ROLL OVER**.

7 The final step is asking him to hold the position when he is on his back with his legs in the air. This is just a matter of asking him to **'STAY'** when in this position. You can physically hold him, reassuring him with praise until he understands.

8 Always release your dog from being 'dead' with an **'OK'**.

9 Once your dog has mastered the trick, you can progress to teaching him to respond from a standing position. Eventually you will be able to 'shoot' your dog in almost any situation, which will really surprise people!

★ TOBY'S TIP ★

'When Katrina first taught me this trick I got a bit confused because there are so many movements involved. The best way to teach us is in stages — so we learn to **SIT, DROP, ROLL OVER** and **STAY**, and then gradually join up the movements. Practise and perfect each command before moving on to the next one.'

TRICK 8
Give a Kiss

This is a way of convincing people that your dog loves you by giving you a kiss on the hand or face when you ask him to. It is very easy to teach as most dogs naturally lick us to let us know that we are their leaders.

WHAT YOU NEED
★ Something tasty like Vegemite

WONDERDOG STEPS

1 Kneel or sit at your dog's height. Smear some Vegemite on your hand (or wherever you want him to kiss you). Only use a tiny amount or you may wind up with a nip.

2 Say **'GIVE ME A KISS'** and tell him what a good boy he is when he licks you. Practise several times with Vegemite, always being very excited when he licks you.

3 Start asking for a kiss without the aid of Vegemite. Reward him with a different food reward if he gives a kiss as requested. He will get the hang of it — repetition, as always, is the key.

TRICK 9
Take a Bow

Toby takes a bow at the end of his stage performances as his way of saying goodbye to his fans. Instead of **TAKE A BOW**, you can substitute **SAY YOUR PRAYERS**. It is exactly the same trick with different words.

WHAT YOU NEED

★ A dog who will **STAY** in the **STAND** position

★ Treats

WONDERDOG STEPS

1 Make your dog **STAND**.

2 Kneel down to your dog's level and support his hindquarters with your arm.

3 With a food treat, encourage his head towards the ground while keeping his hindquarters elevated.

4 Reward him with the treat even if he bends down just a little.

5 Repeat the command **'TAKE A BOW'** each time your dog leans forward.

6 Many dogs try to lie down. Persevere with the hindquarter support and really use the treat for motivation.

7 As soon as you feel your dog understands the movement, command him to **'STAY'** and he should hold the position. Don't remove your supporting arm until you are confident he will stay in the **BOW** position.

8 Always reward him and don't forget to give the release word **'OK'** so he knows when to stop.

9 If he stands up before you ask him to, just reposition him and start again.

10 Include a hand signal. I point my hand towards the ground as I say **'TAKE A BOW'**.

★ **TOBY'S TIP** ★

'Bowing is actually a natural pose for a dog. I **BOW** when I am meeting and greeting other dogs that I want to play with. If you see your dog doing this, you are halfway there — you know that the stance is not difficult for him.'

TRICK 10
Find an Object

Not only can this trick be really cute when you ask your dog to find his favourite toy, but it can also be extremely useful when you ask your dog to find your keys or mobile phone (especially if you misplace them every day like me).

WHAT YOU NEED

★ A dog who **RETRIEVES**   ★ A towel or newspaper
★ Your dog's favourite toy   ★ Strong-smelling treats
like cheese or cabanossi

WONDERDOG STEPS

1 Call your dog and show him your treat. Make him **STAY** and keep his attention while you place the treat under the towel or spread-out newspaper. Don't make it too difficult the first time, as he may lose interest.

2 Release your dog from **STAY** with **'OK'**, and tell him to **'FIND IT'**, encouraging him to help himself to the treat. Make a fuss, telling him what a good boy he is to find the treat.

3 If he has trouble finding the treat, help him out by not covering it completely for the first few attempts.

4 Start covering the treat completely with the towel, making it more difficult to find. Encourage him with urgency in your voice, so he finds it as quickly as possible and doesn't get bored.

5 Start hiding the treat in different locations, near the starting point, so your dog has to sniff it out.

6 Next, have someone cover your dog's eyes while you hide the treat around the house (e.g. in shoes or behind cushions) and ask him to **'FIND IT'**.

7 Once your dog has mastered finding treats, then you can move to objects like his favourite toy or your keys. Use the same principle as with the treats. Allow him to sniff the object in your hand, and command him to **'FIND IT'** after you have hidden it somewhere easy for him.

8 Reward him with a treat when he returns the object to you.

9 Gradually increase the difficulty of the hiding place as you did with the treat.

★ TOBY'S TIP ★

'It is possible to teach us dogs to retrieve a large number of objects, including our own lead — the principles are exactly the same.'

TRICK 11
Find a Person

This doggy equivalent of hide-and-seek is loads of fun.
You can teach your dog to find you or another person.

WHAT YOU NEED

★ A friend or two ★ Some hiding places
(e.g. in a wardrobe, under the bed, behind
some big trees in a park)

WONDERDOG STEPS

1 Stand at one end of the room holding a treat.

2 Get a friend to hold your dog at the other end of the room and ask him to **'FIND KATRINA'**, while you wave your arms and call your dog.

3 Reward your dog with a treat when he gets to you.

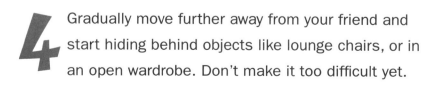

4 Gradually move further away from your friend and start hiding behind objects like lounge chairs, or in an open wardrobe. Don't make it too difficult yet.

Get your friend to release your dog and say **'FIND KATRINA'**. You can call to your dog the first few times, to help.

5 Stop calling your dog yourself and get your friend to give the **'FIND'** command. By now your dog should understand the game and be able to sniff you out.

6 Perfect this trick indoors before venturing to the park and hiding behind trees. In a very short time your dog should be able to sniff you out wherever you are hiding. Most dogs love this game and get really hyped up trying to find their owner.

7 You can start to ask your dog to find other people too, getting him used to different names. After a while you will just have to let your dog have one sniff of someone while you tell him that person's name and he should be able to find him or her.

8 It is important to put lots of encouragement and enthusiasm into your **'FIND'** command. Dogs feed off excitement and will be more willing to please.

★ TOBY'S TIP ★

'I don't just have to find people. I have also learnt to seek out Milly the kitten (my housemate) when she hides in cupboards and drawers. I love it when Katrina tells me to **"FIND MILLY"**, because secretly I enjoy exposing her hiding places — that cat has it too easy!'

TRICK 12
Hug Me

A very simple trick that you can use any time you feel like a cuddle from your dog.

WHAT YOU NEED

★ A dog who can **SIT**

★ A dog familiar with lifting up his front legs

WONDERDOG STEPS

1 Kneel before your dog, who is in the **SIT** position.

2 Gently lift his front paws off the ground, helping him to balance (if your dog **BEGS**, then this should be easy for him).

3 Once he is comfortable, lift both paws onto your shoulders, reassuring him and telling him to **'HUG ME'**. You can help him by supporting him around his body.

4 Give treats if necessary, but I found with Toby that praise and hugs were enough encouragement for him.

TRICK 13
Tail Spin

This trick is great because there is lots of action and movement, and dogs tend to get really excited about having an excuse to jump around and be silly.

WHAT YOU NEED

★ Tasty treats

WONDERDOG STEPS

1 Place your dog in a **STAND** position. Get his attention focused on the treat you are holding. With your dog's nose following the treat, start moving your hand in an arc so that his head and body follow your movement.

2 Tell him to **'SPIN'** and reward him with the treat when he starts moving in a circle. Try to encourage him to put his head as close as possible to his tail when he turns.

3 Start slowly, moving your hand to form a large circle. Gradually make it quicker and smaller. Eventually, it will look like your dog is chasing his tail. Start replacing the treat with a hand movement only.

TRICK 14
Crawl

It is very cute watching Toby crawl along the ground for his toys, so I often use this trick during shoots. It is great to be able to make Toby move a couple of centimetres only, without changing his whole body position or moving other props or animals on the set.

WHAT YOU NEED
★ A dog who **DROPS**   ★ Treats

WONDERDOG STEPS

1 Place your dog in the **DROP** position with his front paws extended in front of him.

2 Hold a treat directly in front of his nose. With your other hand, apply gentle pressure to your dog's back, to deter him from standing up.

3 Move the treat a few centimetres along the floor and encourage your dog to scramble forward to reach it as you say the command **'CRAWL'**.

4 Move your hand further forwards and as soon as your dog moves towards it, praise him by saying **'GOOD BOY'** and giving him the treat.

5 Gradually increase the distance you hold the treat from your dog. Eventually you need to replace the treat with a hand signal.

6 Your dog must learn to keep his hindquarters down. Persevere, taking one step or so at a time, with you gently holding his back end towards the ground.

7 You can help your dog achieve this position by getting a couple of friends to hold up an object your dog can scramble under, like a towel or a piece of cardboard. Always start him in the **DROP** position so he doesn't just dive under the object, but is forced to crawl.

8 Don't forget to use the release word **'OK'** so your dog knows he is allowed to get up and walk normally again.

★ TOBY'S TIP ★

'In the beginning I found this trick rather silly — I used to want to get up and walk. We practised going under things from a **DROP** position, so I soon learnt it was easier to keep my back end down and my belly on the ground.'

TRICK 15
Fetch

A true Wonderdog must be able to retrieve different objects with his mouth, before he can master all the required tricks.

WHAT YOU NEED

★ A soft toy to start or a rolled-up pair of socks (dogs prefer holding soft objects) ★ A long lead or rope ★ A confined area, such as your backyard ★ An excited dog

WONDERDOG STEPS

1 Attach the lead to your dog's collar and attract his attention to the toy by playing with it.

2 When *he* wants to play with it, gently roll the toy along the ground, so that he chases it.

3 Encourage him to pick the toy up, telling him excitedly to **'FETCH'**.

4 When he has the toy in his mouth, tell him to **'COME'**. Using his name will make the command stronger, if necessary: **'COME, TOBY'**.

5 You now have to teach him to keep the toy in his mouth and bring it back to you. If you step towards him, he will probably drop the toy but if you move away from him, he is more likely to come to you.

6 As he does step towards you, give a gentle tug on the lead and encourage him towards you verbally.

7 If he does drop the toy, make a game out of it and quickly send him to **FETCH** it again.

8 Praise him as he gets close to you but don't take the toy off him or he may be reluctant to bring it back to you the next time.

9 Practise these steps, encouraging your dog to chase the toy, **FETCH** it and bring it back to you. Once you are confident he will return to you with the object each time, you can teach him to **GIVE** or **DROP** it and gently remove the object from his mouth. Reward him with a treat.

★ **TOBY'S TIP** ★

'Sometimes we love our toys so much that we don't want to let go — this can usually be solved by bribing us with a tasty treat while you hold the toy with your other hand. The treat will nearly always win over the toy.'

TRICK 16
Carry

This is an extension of **FETCH**, and a very practical one. You can teach your dog to carry pretty much anything in his mouth, including the newspaper, his dog bowl and even your mobile phone.

WHAT YOU NEED

★ A dog who can **FETCH** a variety of toys and objects
★ Soft objects to begin with, such as toys, rolled-up socks or slippers   ★ Treats

WONDERDOG STEPS

1 Practise getting your dog to **FETCH** different objects — he will much prefer soft to hard objects. Make it fun by treating each new object as a game.

2 You must now teach him to **CARRY** each object for a distance. Ask him to **'FETCH'** a soft object and as he brings it to you, walk backwards telling him to **'CARRY'**. Reward him with a treat if he walks even a few paces with it in his mouth.

'CARRY'

3 Gradually increase the distance walked, encouraging him all the way, until you can eventually walk beside him while he is carrying the object in his mouth.

TRICK 17
Put Toys in the Bin

A great trick to show off how smart your dog is — you can have him place objects, like your empty drink can, in the bin, or have him put his own toys away in a basket.

WHAT YOU NEED

★ A dog who will **CARRY** objects and **RELEASE** them on command   ★ A low box or basket
★ An open-top rubbish bin   ★ A soft toy

WONDERDOG STEPS

1 Commence with a soft object and a box or basket that is fairly low to the ground. Send your dog to **'FETCH'** the object as usual, and position yourself so that you are standing next to the box when he returns.

2 As you ask him to **'GIVE'** or **'RELEASE'** the object, in one move take it from his mouth and throw it in the box. Give the command **'RUBBISH'** at the same time.

3 Repeat several times until your dog releases the object when he gets to the box (but always at your command of **'RUBBISH'**). You can help out as necessary by directing the object into the box. Be sure to repeat this step over one or two weeks, to make sure your dog really has grasped it.

4 Once your dog gets used to the basket or box, you can replace it with a bin, and gradually move from soft to harder objects. Make sure you give him plenty of help and encouragement so he understands what his new task is.

5 Eventually, you want to move the bin away from you and be able to command your dog to retrieve an object like an empty can or toy and place it in there.

6 The key word is **'RUBBISH'**. Your dog must learn that this doesn't just mean retrieve the object, but that he must follow through and place it in the bin.

7 Make sure you put lots of enthusiasm into your voice to get your dog excited about the task.

★ TOBY'S TIP ★
'If you are clever, you can learn to bring a Frisbee or ball back from the park and put it in a "special" place, so everyone thinks you are naturally tidy. Hah!'

TRICK 18
Spelling

This was honestly one of the quickest tricks I have taught Toby. It is best to stick to words of three or four letters, like 'Dog' or 'Toby'. This is purely to prevent the audience from getting bored!

WHAT YOU NEED

★ Some large wooden letters from a handicraft shop (you need the letters you would like your dog to spell, plus a few extras) ★ A dog who knows how to **FETCH** and **HOLD** objects ★ A pair of tongs

WONDERDOG STEPS

1 Figure out the word that you want your dog to spell, e.g. 'DOG'.

2 Take only letters D, O and G from the alphabet and handle them so that they are covered in your scent. Your dog will pick out the letters with your scent on them, so make sure you don't touch any letters not required for this trick (hence the tongs).

3 Place the letters D, O, G on the ground and make your dog **FETCH** them, one at a time (but it is unreasonable to expect him to get them in the right order).

4 Once he is bringing the letters D, O, G back to you, add the other letters a few at a time. Handle them only with the tongs. Tell your dog to **'FETCH'**.

TDO P C

5 If he brings back D, O or G, shower him with praise. For any other letter, don't punish but simply say **'UH-UH'** and send him again.

6 Repeat until he *does* bring back one of the desired letters and praise him when he does.

7 He will soon learn that any letter with your scent on it is desirable and he will sniff those out and bring them to you. You can also use smelly food like chicken or cabanossi to rub on the required letters, to help him differentiate them from the others.

★ TOBY'S TIP ★

'You can get us to spell out any word you want, provided you make sure you never touch any of the other letters with your hands, so we can't smell your scent on them. And don't expect us to get the letters in the correct order.'

TRICK 19
Food Refusal

We all know how much dogs love their food, so it is very impressive when your dog has the willpower to not eat food when it is held in front of him. You can do this trick with dinner or with a tempting treat like a biscuit.

WHAT YOU NEED
★ A dog who can **SIT** and **STAY**
★ Food that he enjoys

WONDERDOG STEPS

1 It is best to teach this trick when food is in a bowl, rather than using your hands (they could get bitten). Put only a few pieces of food in the bowl at a time so you can practise several times in one session.

2 You will need a key word like **'LEAVE'** that you will use whenever you want your dog to refuse food. I also use my raised index finger as a hand signal.

3 Ask your dog to **'SIT'** and **'STAY'**.

4 Reinforce **'STAY'** and place his dinner bowl down. Then tell him firmly to **'LEAVE'**. If your dog is good at the **STAY** command, he should wait patiently for your permission to break anyway.

5 Quickly withdraw the bowl back towards your body before he has had time to think about taking the food. Tell him what a good boy he is for staying, and for leaving the food. Then, give him the bowl.

6 If he tries to grab the food give a firm **'UH-UH'** and remove the bowl. Make him **SIT** and **STAY** until *you* give it to him. Basically you are teaching him that if he waits patiently, he will receive the food anyway.

7 Start with only a very short time-span during which you ask him to **'LEAVE'** before allowing him to eat. Gradually increase the time-span. If he does snatch the food from the bowl, just say **'NO!'**

8 Once you are comfortable that he understands the term **LEAVE**, you can start again using treats like biscuits that can be held in your hand (but see Toby's tip).

★ TOBY'S TIP ★

'I learnt this trick when I was a pup and consequently I am very gentle when I take food from Katrina's hand. Not all dogs are so obliging and extra care must be taken when teaching this trick to avoid being bitten. If your dog growls at you, it's best not to persevere.'

TRICK 20
Dance

It's a great party pleaser when your dog has his own disco dance move, which involves him balancing on his hind legs.

WHAT YOU NEED

★ A dog who will **'PLACE'** his front legs on an object and stand on his hind legs ★ Patience

WONDERDOG STEPS

1 Small dogs find it much easier to balance on their hind legs and won't need as much assistance as large dogs. For a small dog, crouch down to his level and hold the treat above his head, so he has to reach for it.

2 Encourage your dog to jump for the treat without allowing him to snatch it. Tell him **'YES'** whenever he gets onto his back legs, but only give him the treat when he holds for a second or more. You can offer your arm for balance if necessary.

3 For medium to large dogs, hold your arm out just above your dog's head.

4 Ask him to **'PLACE'** his two front paws on your arm, which means he is standing (with your help) on his hind legs. You must be ready to provide balance for your dog, as this will be a new experience for him.

5 You must allow him time to figure out his balance with your support. Do this over several sessions and you can encourage him to move a couple of steps forwards and backwards with your help. The more practice he has, the more he will build up the strength he needs in his leg muscles to perform.

6 Don't forget to reward him with a treat or his favourite toy.

7 Start removing your assistance and encourage your dog to start balancing by himself. Reward him with food and remember to praise profusely if he holds the position for even a second.

★ TOBY'S TIP ★

'This trick is definitely easier and safer for little dogs to perform. It is hard for dogs of my size or bigger to balance ourselves and we are more likely get injured. I don't recommend this trick for giant breeds of dogs, like Great Danes or Saint Bernards, or *any dog* that has hip problems.'

Wonderdog Tips

RAISING THE PERFECT PUPPY

1. Choose the breed for you — Be sure to do your homework and choose the right breed of dog to suit your needs and lifestyle. All pups look cute but they grow into dogs of all shapes and sizes with dramatically different needs when it comes to grooming, feeding and exercising. Toby, for example, is a stunning looking dog, but is forever shedding hair everywhere. He also requires a good hour of free running exercise daily, plus plenty of mental stimulation — which he gets by coming out to work with me each day.

2. Choose the right puppy from the litter — Make sure you get a puppy who is bright, alert and responsive to you. He should have clear eyes with no discharge, clean ears and no signs of diarrhoea. Watch him run and play with littermates and make sure he is not limping or injured in any way. Do not fall into the trap of feeling sorry for the runt — these pups are often quieter because they are sickly.

3. Have a set of rules — Be sure everyone in the family agrees as to how the puppy will be raised *before* you bring him home. For example, will he be an indoor or outdoor dog?

Where will he eat and sleep? Everyone must give the same signals to the pup.

4. Supervise your children — Young children mean well and usually think of a puppy as a very exciting new toy. It is important that a puppy has positive experiences with children, so he grows up enjoying their company, rather than being scared of them. Children under five years of age should always sit down to hold a pup and all children should be supervised when playing with any puppy.

5. Puppy-proof your house — Before your puppy comes home, you need to make it a safe environment for him. Remember puppies love to explore everywhere and use their mouths to pick up objects. Items such as electrical cords, batteries, pesticides, human medication, razors, plants and cleaning products must be put out of reach.

6. Visit the vet — Your puppy should have had his first vaccination before you bring him home, but will still need another couple of shots because his immune system is immature and he is at great risk of contracting serious viral diseases. Your vet will also give your puppy a complete physical exam and discuss other issues, like worming, flea control, and training.

7. Worm regularly — Puppies should be wormed every two weeks for internal parasites such as roundworm, hookworm, tapeworm and whipworm. Worm adult dogs at least every three months for life. Worm tablets are available from vets, pet stores and supermarkets. Be sure to buy an 'all-wormer'.

8. Provide things to chew — It is natural for puppies to chew a lot while they are teething, and Toby was no exception. He munched everything he could get his mouth around, including soap, my favourite shoes and my flatmate's futon mattress. The more chewy toys I gave him, like rawhide chews and rope bones, the safer my belongings were and the happier he was.

9. Attend puppy classes — The period from 8 to 16 weeks in a puppy's life is the most important time for him to learn how to socialise and interact with other dogs and cats as well as people. I highly recommend puppy classes, which are held at veterinary clinics over a three to four week period and teach puppies (and owners) important social skills as well as basic health care and training techniques.

10. Handle your puppy daily — I cannot emphasise enough how important it is to handle your puppy daily and get him used to being restrained by you. Touch and handle his feet, tail and ears, and get your puppy used to having his mouth opened. Always reassure and reward him constantly so that he learns to not be at all threatened by your touch. Spending a few minutes each day handling a puppy is much easier than struggling to touch an adult dog.

KEEPING YOUR DOG HEALTHY

1. Vaccinations — It is essential that your dog receives a yearly vaccination booster to prevent him catching certain viral diseases that can cause serious illness or even death. Your annual visit to the vet is also the time when you can discuss any problems and have your pet's health fully checked out.

2. Intestinal worms — It is important to worm your adult dog with an 'all-wormer' every three months. Worms can be transmitted in various ways, from ingesting fleas and faeces to eating contaminated meat. Symptoms include diarrhoea, weight loss, general poor appearance, a pot belly and occasional vomiting.

3. Heartworm — Heartworm is a disease transmitted by mosquitoes and is deadly if left untreated. Adult heartworms infect the heart, where they grow and block the heart, causing disease and death. A monthly tablet is all that it takes to prevent a heartworm infection and unnecessary heartache. There are now injections available too.

4. Feeding — Like humans, a dog needs a balanced diet and your vet will discuss various feeding options. I feed Toby a good quality, balanced, commercial dry food, combined with low fat foods like pasta, rice and chicken. He also gets a beef marrowbone to munch on every week — not only are these great for his teeth, they keep him occupied for hours.

5. Grooming — All dogs require some grooming — how much will depend on the breed. I bathe Toby once every two to three weeks and give him a thorough brushing twice a week. I also trim the hair between his toes and on his belly. Grooming time is quality time to spend with your dog and gives you a chance to check him over for cuts, lumps and bumps.

6. Training — A dog who has basic obedience training is a delightful dog to be around. And although it is much easier to train a puppy, it is never too late to begin training your adult dog. If you are willing to invest some of your precious time in doggy training school, you will be rewarded many times over with the pleasure and satisfaction it brings in return.

7. Desexing — Unless you are planning on breeding from your dog, I recommend desexing from six months of age. This will prevent unwanted pregnancies and embarrassing sexual behaviour. It will also decrease the risk of mammary cancer in female dogs and prostate cancer in males.

8. Nails — A dog's nails continue to grow and unless he is pounding the pavements daily, it is probable they will need regular trimming. The key is to cut only the tip of the nail, avoiding the blood vessel inside (called the quick). You can see the quick inside light coloured nails, but cannot see it in dark nails — so be careful.

9. Dental care — Regular attention should be given to dental care, as gum disease is very common in dogs. Some hard dry food should be included in your dog's diet as this will help clean his teeth. Fresh marrowbones once or twice a week also help keep teeth and gums in tiptop shape. You can teach your dog to tolerate having his teeth brushed regularly — this is best taught from puppyhood.

10. Mental health — This is very important. A healthy dog is one who feels he is an important part of the pack and who receives plenty of mental stimulation and positive praise. A dog really only wants to please you, and the least you can do is provide an environment in which he can thrive.

KEEPING YOUR DOG FIT

1. Walking — Power walking with your dog is not just good for him, but you get the benefits as well. You may find it easier to motivate yourself if you have a regular walk organised with a friend. When walking on the street, always keep your dog on a lead.

2. Play Kong — Toby's personal favourite. Kongs are rubber toys that dogs find impossible to chew through. There is one attached to a nylon rope that allows you to throw it so much further than you could ever throw a ball. I only have to mention the word 'Kong' in my house and Toby goes into a frenzy of excitement.

3. Tennis racket and ball — This is a great way to get your dog running, while you can be lazy and stay in one spot — provided your dog returns the ball to you.

4. Play Frisbee — One of Toby's favourite sports, but I am always cautious not to let him jump too high, as the impact of landing on his hind legs can cause damage to the ligaments of the knee. Make sure you use a soft dog Frisbee to avoid broken teeth!

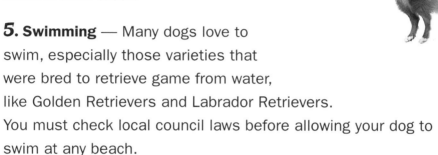

5. Swimming — Many dogs love to swim, especially those varieties that were bred to retrieve game from water, like Golden Retrievers and Labrador Retrievers. You must check local council laws before allowing your dog to swim at any beach.

6. Agility clubs — Around the country, there are agility clubs with classes for beginners through to advanced. These activities are both mentally and physically stimulating and involve the dog learning to do a course involving jumps, tunnels and climbing apparatus. Dogs that compete do so against time. Look for agility clubs in the *Yellow Pages*.

7. Dog walkers — If you don't think your dog is getting enough exercise, pay a 'dog walker' to pick up your dog and exercise him for you. Up to six dogs are walked at a time and

the dogs have great fun playing together for an hour or so. It is a good idea to accompany the walker for the first time to make sure you are comfortable with his or her dog handling skills.

8. Working dog weekends — These are weekends away in the country for working dogs, like Toby, who live in the city. The city slicker dog gets lessons in working sheep and by the end of the weekend most dogs with the instinct to herd are happily rounding up the sheep. Great exercise for a working dog!

9. Sled dog racing — Great for Alaskan Malamutes and Siberian Huskies, who were originally bred for pulling sleds in the snow. In Australia there are also sled events on dirt courses. The Malamute or Siberian Husky club can give you more information.

10. Flyball — This is a really exciting sport for both dogs and owners. This game is a relay race with teams of four dogs.

Each dog must jump over a series of hurdles, step on a trigger that releases a tennis ball and carry that ball back over the hurdles to the next dog who is eagerly awaiting his turn. Several teams race at once and the first team to finish wins the heat. This is a great sport for dogs who love balls and enjoy jumping. (For more information, contact the Australian Flyball Association at www.flyball.org.au)

FACTS ABOUT TOBY

1. Toby was bred at Bordercheck Kennels on a beautiful property in Wildesmeadow, NSW. His mother was a chocolate Border Collie, and his father was a black Border Collie. Ninety-five per cent of Border Collies are black and white, which makes Toby rather rare.

2. Toby comes from working stock and he still has a strong urge to round up sheep. He also likes to round up soccer games and people who are trying to have a relaxing game of tennis.

3. Toby sleeps on an orthopaedic dog bed and really uses the lamb's wool pillow to rest his head on (provided Milly the cat is not already there).

4. Toby has a weird obsession with birds in cages. He does not want to hurt them, but sits under their cage and stares all day. He ignores all other birds.

5. He really loves to swim and has been known to sneak off quietly on shoots, jump into a nearby swimming pool and trot back like nothing has happened. He is always the first dog to lie in a muddy puddle and will do so at any opportunity.

6. He is not allowed to sleep on my bed, but I often find a warm patch and suspicious-looking hairs on my doona cover on returning home.

7. His best friend is an eight-year-old Blue Heeler called Hannah. He gets so excited when we turn up at her place that he wants to jump out the car window. I know he really must love her because she is the only dog in the country who is allowed to steal his Frisbee without a tantrum.

8. Toby has a terrible body hair problem — it ends up all over everything (the lounge, my clothes, my car. . .). Lucky I love him.

9. When Toby comes to me and begs for no reason at all, I always know there must really be a reason and that he has probably raided the rubbish bin again. . . Even Wonderdogs can be naughty sometimes.

10 Toby accompanies me most days to my shoots but when I travel interstate he hangs out with his personal dog trainer, Steve Austin. Steve has trained many TV and movie star dogs in his time and assures me that Toby is as smart as the best of them. I like to hear that because I am as proud as a dog owner could be.

11 Toby was a little bit put out when I brought home Milly the Burmilla kitten. He was used to being the only pet in the house, and now this tiny little kitten wanted to take over his spot. Now, however, Toby and Milly are the best of friends, and sometimes Toby even lets her share his lamb's wool pillow.

12 If Toby misses out on having a

run for some reason (like a hailstorm), he potters around, dropping toys and socks at my feet all night.

13 Toby has two step-brothers, Benny and Bowie, who are both Dalmatians. Ever since meeting them, he loves all Dalmatians, and always heads straight for them if he sees them in the park, hoping to play.

FACTS ABOUT DOGS

1. All dogs are descended from the wolf. It is believed they were domesticated around 12,000 years ago, then bred over the centuries for different purposes, like herding or hunting.

2. The smallest dog in the world is the Chihuahua, the tallest is the Irish Wolfhound and the heaviest is the Saint Bernard.

3. There are over four million households in Australia with at least one dog. In fact, Australia has one of the highest rates of dog ownership per capita in the world.

4. Some 85 per cent of dog owners agree that their dog is part of the family, like a child.

5. Dog owners visit the doctor less often than non-dog owners. Research has shown that people who own pets have lower risk of heart disease, lower blood pressure and cholesterol. And taking your dog for a walk every day keeps you healthy.

6. The dog serves us in many ways other than just as a companion — guide dogs, police dogs, 'sniffer' dogs, guard dogs and therapy dogs, to name a few.

7. A dog's sense of smell is its most highly developed sense, allowing them to smell things undetectable to us. This is because they have thousands more receptors in their nasal tissue, and is the reason dogs are used to detect missing persons, bombs and illegal substances.

8. Dogs see better than humans in poor light, but not as well in bright light. They can't see distances well but are attuned to movement.

9. A dog has much better hearing than us. They can register sounds of up to 35,000 vibrations per second whilst we only hear around 20,000 vibrations per second. Silent whistles used to train dogs produce sound at 25,000 vibrations per second, which is easy for dogs to hear but too high for us.

10. Dogs really need a variety of different exercises to prevent them from getting bored. They love new sights, smells and experiences.

SUMMERTIME

1. Always have fresh water available. Use heavy bowls, not plastic ones that can be easily knocked over. Leave out two bowls in case one gets finished.

2. You must be sure that there is some shade in the yard throughout the day.

3. Never leave your dog in your car, even for a few minutes. A dog can die in five minutes on a hot day. Even with the windows down, the heat can quickly rise to deadly levels.

4. Pavements and roads can get extremely hot and burn the pads on your dog's paws. Stick to cooler grassy areas and avoid walking in the heat of the day.

5. Dogs also suffer from skin cancer and sunburn. This is most common in white dogs or dogs with pink skin on their noses and ears. Keep dogs out of the sun between 11.00 a.m. and 3.00 p.m.

Try applying zinc to the nose or use a protective sunsuit if your dog likes to lie belly up.

6. Many pets suffer from allergies to grasses and wandering Jew in summer, resulting in red, itchy skin. You must remove the cause (which is often difficult to isolate).

7. Fleas thrive in warm, moist climates and can be a terrible summer problem for both dog and owner. These days, they are controllable with topical products and thorough cleaning of the dog's environment, including its bedding, your furniture and the floorboards. Your vet can give you more information.

8. Paralysis ticks are found on the eastern seaboard from northern Queensland to northern Victoria. Use a preventative like drop products which are applied to the back of the neck. Check your dog daily, particularly his ears and between his toes. If you find a tick, remove it with tweezers, making sure you pull out the mouthparts as well.

9. Many dogs drown in swimming pools in summer. Most dogs can swim but not all can find their way out of the pool, so make sure you keep your pool fenced.

DOG SAFETY

1. Never feed your dog cooked bones, as these can splinter and get caught in his mouth.

2. Check your garden for poisonous plants like oleander. Although it is unlikely that an adult dog would eat the plant, puppies may well chew on it. The bulbs of daffodils, jonquils and tulips are also poisonous.

3. Train your dog to wear a harness when travelling in a car. In the case of an accident, you don't want him to be a flying missile. It is the law that dogs riding in cars must be tethered.

4. As much as dogs love chasing sticks, sticks can impale the roof of your dog's mouth. Take your own toys out with you, but if you must throw a stick, allow it to land before letting your dog chase after it.

5. Always keep your dog on a lead when you take him to the vet clinic

— you just never know what other animals will be sitting in the waiting room.

6. Never tie your dog up with a lead attached to a check chain. Should he pull back or get into a fight, he could strangle himself.

7. Keep dogs away from insecticides, fertilisers, snail bait, and also away from areas of the garden that have been sprayed with chemical fertiliser.

8. Don't give your dog human medications unless specifically prescribed by your vet. A dog's body metabolises chemicals differently to the way the human body does.

9. Be careful when renovating old houses, as dogs can get poisoned from lead paint.

10. Chocolate and onions can be toxic to dogs so avoid letting your dog eat them, even accidentally.

CARING FOR YOUR OLDER DOG

1. It is essential that your older dog visits the vet regularly to check for signs of diseases like arthritis, heart disease, cancer or kidney failure. Many diseases can be managed if caught early.

2. Older dogs sometimes appear to get grumpy, but this is often because their eyesight and hearing is failing and sudden sounds and movements startle them.

3. Provide a warm comfy bed away from draughts.

4. Older dogs can't walk up and down stairs like they used to or jump up onto the furniture (even if this is allowed!). You can help them out by providing a ramp.

5. As dogs age, they prefer eating soft food, which is easier to chew. This leads to gum and tooth disease, but you can avoid this by brushing your dog's teeth and gums a couple of times a week. Ask your vet how to do this. You can get special toothbrushes for dogs and even meat-flavoured toothpaste. Don't use human toothpaste as it is too acidic.

6. An older dog is unlikely to groom himself properly. You should brush your dog thoroughly a couple of times a week. This not only feels good for your dog and stimulates his skin, but gives you an opportunity to check him over for any lumps.

7. A dog's bladder is not as strong in his older years and he will need the opportunity to eliminate more frequently.

8. Elderly dogs are not as energetic as young dogs, but that doesn't mean that they don't need some exercise. Dogs of any age thrive on the smells and sounds of the outdoors — just keep the pace slow and gentle.

9. If your dog loves other dogs, then getting a younger playmate may be just the thing to make him feel a few years younger.

10. Give loads of love. Your dog has been your faithful companion for many years and has given you unconditional love. During his twilight years, it is up to you to return this.

HOLIDAYING WITH YOUR DOG

1. Attach an ID tag with the phone number of where you are staying (or your mobile number) to your dog's collar. Your home number is no good as you won't be there to answer.

2. Before leaving home, check the place you are staying at will allow your dog. Remember, dogs are not permitted in National Parks or on many beaches.

3. If travelling by car, make your dog wear a harness. These clip into the seatbelt and prevent your dog from becoming a flying missile should you have an accident.

4. Always keep your dog on a lead in unfamiliar surroundings. You cannot predict his response to the sounds and smells of new territory.

5. While travelling in the car, make sure you have regular breaks so that your dog can do his doggy business, stretch his legs and have some water.

6. If travelling interstate, air travel is the best option. Pre-book your dog's flight and check him in an hour before departure for domestic flights. You will need to hire or buy a travel cage or crate.

7. Dogs like a secure, familiar place to sleep. Using your car as a temporary kennel is not recommended as it is not insulated. And it's unlikely you will hear if there are problems.

8. Pack a first-aid kit. Be aware of potential dangers in the area you are visiting, such as snakes, ticks and jellyfish, and take appropriate precautions.

9. Don't assume you will be able to get your usual dog food when on holiday. Dogs often get tummy upsets when their diet is suddenly changed, so take your own supplies.

10. Like humans, dogs and especially pups can get carsick. It is best to not feed your dog immediately before you set out, to avoid any unpleasant accidents while travelling.

REWARD AND DISCIPLINE

1. Be consistent! It is essential that all family members agree to use the same training techniques. This includes words that you will use, hand signals and punishment. It is no use teaching your dog not to sleep on the couch if the rest of the household allows him to.

2. You must learn to reward your dog the second he does whatever you have asked him to do. A dog thinks for the moment and quickly connects what he is doing with the reward. If you delay the reward, he will think it is for the next action.

3. The same applies to punishment — there is absolutely no point in punishing a dog after the act. You must discipline as your dog performs the act. Dogs don't remember like humans do — they work in the present so won't connect the punishment with something that happened in the past. A classic example is rubbing a puppy's nose in its business — the puppy won't understand what it has done and just become afraid of you. However, if you catch him 'in the act' and use a scowl in your voice, he will make the connection between the act and your disapproval.

4. Punishment should not be physical — dogs feel pain just like we do. Instead, use a scowl in your voice or a firm **'NO!'**. Not only can physical punishment injure your dog, but it will make him afraid of you and you may never get back his trust.

5. Often the best lesson for your dog is for him to be ignored. A lot of annoying behaviour is just attention seeking by your dog, such as jumping up at the door. If you ignore him, he will probably stop the behaviour. Always shower your dog with praise when he does the right thing.

6. A 'sin-bin' is useful if a dog or puppy is being consistently naughty. This is a confined area where you can put the animal to calm down for 10 minutes or so. Never make this an area that he must enjoy for other activities, but rather an area of isolation for a short period only.

7. When teaching anything new, you should reward your dog with a food treat each time he performs the desired act. Gradually cut down the food rewards and replace them with verbal praise. You don't want your dog to be dependent on food treats as this devalues the power of the food. It is better to have him unsure about when he will receive the treat, so he remains keen and hopeful.

8. When teaching anything new always quit while you are ahead. Make sure you stop and reward your dog when all is going well. Don't push until your dog stops learning, as this will only end the lesson on a down note. Training must always be fun.

9. Never underestimate the power of a favourite toy as a reward. I always give Toby his Kong toy at the end of a training session, so that he knows his lessons are over and he can start having fun.

10. Don't forget that your dog really just wants to please you. Always tell him when he is being a good boy — for example, if he is lying down patiently or not hanging around the dining table — so that he is encouraged to do the right thing.